Does Grandma Have an Elmo Elephant Jungle Kit?

LAURA JOFFE NUMEROFF

Greenwillow
Read-alone

GREENWILLOW BOOKS
New York

Published by Greenwillow Books, A Division of William Morrow & Company, Inc.
105 Madison Avenue, New York, N.Y. 10016
Printed in the United States of America   First Edition   10   9   8   7   6   5   4   3   2   1
Color separations by William Joffe Numeroff

Library of Congress Cataloging in Publication Data
Numeroff, Laura Joffe.   Does grandma have an Elmo Elephant jungle kit?
(Greenwillow read-alone books)   Summary: Donald is worried that there'll be nothing to do at his
grandparents' house during a weekend visit and wants to take all his toys along.   [1. Grandparents—Fiction]
I. Title.   PZ7.N964Do   [E]   79-16301   ISBN 0-688-80249-4   ISBN 0-688-84249-6 lib. bdg.

For Libby and Ava

Donald was going to spend
the weekend with his grandparents.
It was the first time
he was going by himself.
"You're not moving to Grandma's,"
Donald's mother said.
"You're only going for three days."
Donald's room looked as if
a tornado had hit it.

"Does Grandma have
an Elmo Elephant Jungle Kit,"
he asked,
"and a Captain Bob Fire Helmet?"
"I'm not sure," she said.
"So if I don't take them with me,
there won't be anything
for me to do,"
he explained.

"Oh, Donald," she said,
as she left the room,
"I'm sure there will be
plenty to do at Grandma's."

Donald followed his mother
into the kitchen.
"Can I make
a peanut butter
sandwich?"
he asked.

"But you just had lunch,"
his mother said.
"This is to take along,"
Donald said.
"I'm sure Grandma has plenty
of food," his mother told him.
"She might not have any
peanut butter," said Donald.

Then the doorbell rang.

"Oh, no!" Donald moaned.

"I'm not even halfway finished
with packing.

I hope Grandma can wait."

But it wasn't Grandma
who was at the door.
It was Alan and Brenda,
two of Donald's friends.

"Come into my room," he said.

"I've got to finish packing."

"Are you running away?"

Alan asked.

"No, I'm just going
to my grandma's
for the weekend,"
Donald told him.

"You'll need an army to carry
all of that," said Brenda.
"Army?" said Donald.
"That reminds me.
I forgot my plastic soldiers."

Donald tried stuffing them
into his picnic basket.
But he still didn't have room
for his magic kit
with the seven tricks in it.

"I've got to have this with me,"
Donald said.
He took everything out
that he had just packed.
"If I don't take all of this,
there won't be anything
for me to do," he said.
"I know what you mean,"
Brenda said.
"I never have anything to do
at my grandma's."

Just then Donald's mother
came into the room.
"Grandma's downstairs
and she's double-parked.
You'd better just take
what you have ready,"
she said.
She grabbed
his suitcase
and hurried
him out.

Alan and Brenda
yelled good-bye
as he ran out the door.

"Well, Donald," Grandma said

when he got into the car,

"I hope you are ready

for a busy weekend."

Busy? Donald thought,

I didn't bring a single thing

to play with.

"Do you think I could

call home from your house?"

he asked.

"I forgot something

and maybe my mother

could bring it."

"Don't worry," Grandma said,
"I'm sure we'll have
everything you'll need."

Grandpa showed Donald his room.

There was a big package
on the bed.
"We got you a surprise,"
Grandpa said.

Donald unwrapped the package.

"Oh, wow!" he said.

"A magic kit just like mine!
Only this one is better.
It has twenty tricks."

"Grandpa couldn't wait
until you got here.
He just loves magic,"
Grandma said.

"Oh, thank you,"
said Donald. "So do I."

"Now, let's make a plan,"
said Grandma.
"Would you like to go
to the aquarium today?"
Grandpa was studying
the magic kit.
"The trick with the frog
looks very interesting,"
he said.

"–or we could go to the zoo,"
Grandma said.
"–and so does the trick
with the magic mirror,"
said Grandpa.
"–or we could have a picnic
by the waterfall,"
Grandma suggested.

Donald looked from Grandma

to Grandpa.

He had never been to the aquarium.

But he did want to try the trick

with the disappearing frog.

"If we go to the aquarium,
can we play with
the magic kit later?"
he asked.
"Of course," said Grandma.

They went to the aquarium.

Donald's favorite fish
was the lion fish.

"I don't know why

they call it that," said Grandpa.

"I didn't hear it roar."

Everyone laughed.

They all had a wonderful time.

When they got home,

Donald helped Grandma

make dinner.

They roasted marshmallows
in the fireplace for dessert.
Before Donald knew it,
it was time for bed.

The next day, after breakfast,
Grandma suggested that
they go for a walk by the lake.
Grandpa wanted to try
the eraser trick.

It was hard for Donald to decide.

"Let's go to the lake now,"

Grandma said.

"It is so lovely in the morning.

You can play with the kit later."

"Sounds good to me,"

said Grandpa.

"Me, too," said Donald.

They took a long walk by the lake.

They fed the ducks

and Grandpa showed Donald

how to skip stones.

After lunch,

Grandpa had to go out.

"Let's make puppets,"

Grandma said.

She and Donald made puppets

with socks and buttons.

Donald called his Muffin.
Grandma called hers Morris.
When Grandpa came home,
they put on a puppet show
for him.

Then Donald tried
one of the magic tricks.
But Grandpa fell asleep
before Donald could get
the coin to disappear.

The next day, they drove
to a little waterfall.
They had a picnic
of peanut butter sandwiches,
lemonade, and bananas.
And they talked about
lots of interesting things.

As they were driving
Donald home that evening,
Grandpa said,
"We hardly got to use
the magic kit."

"That's okay," said Donald.

"You and Grandma

can keep it at your house

and we can play with it

next time I come."

"I hope it will be soon,"

said Grandpa.

"Me, too," said Donald.

"Did you have a good time?"
his father asked
when Donald got home.
"Yes," said Donald.
"We didn't even have time
to play with the magic kit
Grandpa bought me.
Can I go again soon?"

"Of course,"

said his mother.

"But right now,

get ready for bed.

Then you can tell us

all about the things you did."

"Oh, good," said Donald.

"That will take all night!"

LAURA JOFFE NUMEROFF
grew up in Brooklyn, New York. Her interest in the
arts was nurtured at home from childhood on, and for
the multi-talented Laura the choice between music
and art as a career was not an easy one.

She is a graduate of Pratt Institute, and the author-
artist of *Phoebe Dexter Has Harriet Peterson's Sniffles* and
Amy for Short, and the co-author (with her sister Alice
Richter) and illustrator of *You Can't Put Braces on Spaces*
and *Emily's Bunch*.